Tom Percival grew up in a remote and beautiful part of south Shropshire. It was so remote that he lived in a small caravan without mains electricity or any sensible form of heating. He thinks he's probably one of the few people in his peer group to have learned to read by gas lamp.

Having established a career as a picture-book author and illustrator, Little Legends is Tom's first chapter-book series for young readers. The idea for Little Legends was developed by Tom with Made in Me, a digital studio exploring new ways for technology and storytelling to inspire the next generation.

MACMILLAN CHILDREN'S BOOKS

*This book is dedicated to my brother, Hugh,
for all our childhood adventures*

First published 2016 by Macmillan Children's Books
an imprint of Pan Macmillan
20 New Wharf Road, London N1 9RR
Associated companies throughout the world
www.panmacmillan.com

ISBN 978-1-4472-9211-1

1 3 5 7 9 8 6 4 2

A CIP catalogue record for this book is available from the British Library.

Printed and bound by CPI Group (UK) Ltd, Croydon CR0 4YY

Contents

1

A Storm Brewing

Red, Anansi, Rapunzel, Jack and his magical talking hen, Betsy, were sitting beneath the leafy branches of the Story Tree in the middle of Tale Town.

The afternoon sun beat down upon them and the air was thick and heavy. Out to sea storm clouds were gathering – the weather wouldn't hold for long.

'What do you think Hansel and

Gretel are up to?' asked Red.

'They said they were going camping with their dad,' said Rapunzel.

'**Whaaaat?**' squawked Betsy, rolling her eyes. Although she was a talking hen, Betsy could only say the word '**What**' – but somehow her friends always knew what she meant.

Jack frowned. 'It is *weird*, isn't it?' he said. 'They go off on these trips to the woods with their dad, and then we don't see them for weeks! But I saw their dad in town just this morning with *another* new wife – and she's even worse than the last one. He was buying her a diamond-covered toilet-roll holder and looked *really* miserable.'

They fell silent. Life in Tale Town

was always *slightly* unusual, but what else would you expect in a place where stories literally grew on trees?

The Story Tree was the reason that Tale Town got its name. On its branches grew every story that had ever been told near it. To 'read' the stories, all you had to do was run your finger along any branch or leaf and the tale would spring to life in your head. All the children had at least one or two stories growing on the Story Tree – even Anansi, who hadn't been living there very long.

'So Anansi, how's your uncle Rufaro doing?' asked Rapunzel. 'Any news?'

'Well, he still looks like a troll,' replied Anansi. 'So he's still living in that stinking cave in the woods, away from all his friends and family, surviving on scraps of food, and water from that smelly pond.'

'Hmm,' replied Rapunzel. 'So not

that great, then?'

'Not really,' said Anansi with a sigh.

It had been well over a year since almost all of Anansi's family had been cursed to look, sound and smell like trolls. Only Anansi and his father still looked human. Nobody knew how it had happened, or why. More worryingly, nobody had the slightest clue how to turn them back. Even *more* worryingly, the people of Tale Town and the trolls had been at war for as long as anyone could remember. Without a cure, his family would never be able to come home.

'And what about your mum?' asked Jack. 'Is she still on her way here?'

Anansi brightened. 'Yeah, she should arrive any day now! Dad sorted out a ticket on a boat from Far Far Away.' He paused. 'Well, I say a "ticket" . . . Let's just say she's on a boat.'

'Don't worry, Anansi,' said Red, patting him on the arm, 'I just know that Rufaro will be able to find a cure.'

'I guess so,' replied Anansi, but he didn't sound hopeful.

A large raindrop landed with a puff of dust on the dry ground and Jack glanced up.

'Looks like it's about to—'

He was interrupted by a crash of thunder as huge, fat raindrops fell all around them. Everybody sprang to their feet and ran for cover.

———◆◆———

The captain had already given the order to abandon ship. The boat had been thrown on to a series of jagged rocks a mile or so from Tale Town and was taking on water. As the last of the lifeboats were lowered, a deep voice boomed from a huge box in the hold.

'Hello? Is there anybody there? I don't want to alarm you, but my feet are getting wet, and I just wondered if everything was OK? The boat's not sinking, is it?'

There was no response. By now water was halfway up the side of the crate which was printed with the words:

TAKE CARE.
ENCHANTED
SPINNING WHEELS –
MAY CAUSE DROWSINESS

'*Yiiikes!*' squealed the voice as the water rose higher.

It was hard to imagine such a deep and gravelly voice squealing, but *somehow* it managed it.

'I'm going to come out now,' the voice continued. 'But just to warn you . . . I look a *teeny* bit like a troll. But I'm not *really* a troll! So, no spears or swords, right? Agreed?'

Again there was no answer.

The voice in the box muttered, 'Here we go then . . .' and with a crash the crate exploded outward, revealing a very large, very trolly-looking *troll*.

The troll glanced around and realized that the ship definitely *was* sinking. It searched through its pockets until it found what it was looking for – a bright yellow bottle – then it scrambled up the steps towards the deck and leaped up the mast, climbing as fast as it could until it reached the crow's nest. Shutting its eyes in concentration, the troll whispered a spell into the yellow bottle – then sealed it with a cork and flung it far out into the towering waves.

Seconds later, the troll fell into the churning water, leaving a splash of white spray that was immediately swallowed up in the darkness of the storm.

2
Message in a Bottle

The next day, all anyone could talk about was the shipwreck. Red, Jack, Rapunzel, Anansi and Betsy were walking to the beach to see if anything exciting had washed up.

Red shuddered. 'I'm glad everyone made it back to shore,' she said. 'It must have been terrifying!'

'I know!' exclaimed Rapunzel, stroking her incredibly long plaits.

'Imagine having to wash all that salt water out of your hair!'

'That's not *exactly* what I meant . . .' began Red, but before she had a chance to finish, Old Bert wheeled his cart round the corner. Red groaned. She didn't like seafood at the best of times, and Old Bert's seafood-snack cart smelled *very* fishy.

'Mornin', small fry!' Old Bert said with a toothy grin. 'Which of me salty snacks will you be 'avin' today?'

Red looked around and realized her friends had vanished as quickly as Old Bert had appeared. She could see Jack's feet poking out from underneath a bush, while Betsy was pretending to be the figurehead on a boat.

'The thing is . . .' replied Red, 'I've only just had breakfast, so I'm, er, kind of full.'

Old Bert chuckled. 'Always room for a pot of me finest squid rings!' he said, pulling out a grubby jar.

'*Ewwww!*' exclaimed Red. 'I mean, erm . . . I've not got enough money.'

Bert's eyes narrowed. 'Well, I do

'ave some old fish tails going cheap —
not even rotten yet — 'ow many d'yer
want?'

'Yes . . . *but* . . . I'm allergic to fish
tails!'

'*Really?*' asked Bert, his needle-sharp
eyes boring into her. 'Just last week I
sold you eight of 'em!'

'I know!' continued Red, shivering at
the memory. 'I think that was what did
it.'

A cunning smile stretched across Bert's
face. 'As it happens I'm also sellin' ice
cream today,' he said. 'How does that
grab yer?'

'Really?' asked Red, 'Well, I probably
could eat an ice cream . . .'

Before Red knew what had

happened, all her money was gone, she was holding an ice cream and Old Bert was hobbling off whistling a tuneless sea shanty.

Red stood waiting on the path as, one by one, her friends reappeared.

'Oh, *hello*. Nice of you to join me!' she said, scowling. 'I *know* you think Old Bert's always tricking me into buying some horrid seafood thing, but not today!' She waved the crumpled ice-cream cone at them triumphantly. 'So *you* all missed out!'

'WHAaAT?' squawked Betsy, looking suspicious.

'Oh, come *on*, Betsy!' exclaimed Red. 'Ice cream is ice cream, it'll be lovely!'

And with that she ripped off the packaging and took a huge bite.

'*GAhhhHhh!*' coughed Red. She looked in horror at the ice cream, over to her friends, and finally at the packaging in her hand. The label was clear for everyone to see:

OLD BERT'S EEL-EYE ICE CREAM

'*Why would anyone do that?*' cried Red, throwing the ice cream in a bin and scraping at her tongue with her fingernails.

'Red, Bert *always* tricks you into buying something, and it's *always* horrible,' said Anansi. 'Maybe you shouldn't be so trusting?'

Red glared at him. 'If *I* hadn't trusted *you* when you first arrived in Tale Town, we wouldn't all be friends now, would we?'

Anansi looked at her. 'I know,' he said. 'And I'm really glad you did, but –'

'Hey, look at that!' Rapunzel interrupted, pointing towards the shoreline.

Bobbing against the sand was a yellow bottle filled with a strange glowing mist. When the children got nearer, the bottle spun around until it was pointing towards them. Then it hopped up out of the sea and started rolling up the beach.

'Whoa!' said Red as the bottle came to a stop at their feet. 'It's a message in a bottle!'

'But who's it for?' wondered Jack.

They peered at the bottle and the mist inside formed into different shapes, gradually becoming clearer and clearer:

Anansi looked nervous as he bent to pick up the bottle and slowly pulled out the cork. As he did, the beach and his friends faded away. Anansi looked around in confusion. He was up in the crow's nest of a ship, late at night. Rain

fell all around him, but he couldn't feel
a thing. In front of him was a troll that
he recognized – *it was his mother!*

Anansi tried to hug her, but his arms
passed right through her.

Anansi's mother stared straight ahead and spoke quickly:

'Anansi, my darling! The ship is sinking! I'm close to Tale Town and can see an island that I can swim to — there is a mountain on it that looks like a squirrel's nose. I'll meet you there, at the base of the mountain, where the forest ends. Come as soon as you can. I love you, Anansi, stay safe!'

The scene melted away and Anansi found himself back on the beach, surrounded by his friends.

'Well?' asked Jack expectantly. 'What was the message? Who was it from?'

'My mum,' said Anansi. 'And we need to find a boat that'll take us to Squirrel-Nose Island — *right now!*'

3

The Huntsman's Picnic

*B*y lunchtime, Red, Anansi, Jack and Betsy were on board Tale Town's most luxurious cruise liner – the *Silver Spoon*. Because Rapunzel's parents were the King and Queen, she could get tickets for *anything* – being a princess *was* pretty handy sometimes.

'WHAaAT?' squawked Betsy loudly, flapping a wing towards the horizon.

'Well, it's called Squirrel-Nose Island

because that big mountain looks like a squirrel's nose,' replied Jack.

'Whaaaat?'

'You're right,' said Jack. 'Maybe it does look a bit more like a fox's nose, but you couldn't call it "Fox-Nose Island", could you? That would just be silly!'

Betsy rolled her eyes.

'We're nearly there!' interrupted Anansi. 'Let's go on deck.'

The cabin crew looked on in surprise as two scruffy boys, an even scruffier chicken, the royal princess and a girl in a bright red hood dashed out of the Royal Cabin. Still, they all had valid tickets (even the chicken), so the captain

bowed as low as he could, although he
did feel that standards were *definitely*
slipping.

They scrambled off the boat as
quickly as they could and were soon
running through the thick woodland.

'Hurry up!' shouted Anansi as Jack,
Rapunzel and Red puffed and panted
behind him. The path had narrowed to
a single track winding upward through
the trees with a steep drop down to the
valley below.

Even Betsy was doing the fastest
jump–hop–wing-flap–glide that she
could, but she didn't look happy about
it. Hens aren't known for their athletic
ability, even magical ones.

There was a stone in Red's shoe and it was getting really annoying. She stopped for a moment to shake it out, but just as she was retying her shoe the lace snapped. 'Typical!' Red muttered as she fished around in her pockets for some string. But by the time she had fixed her laces, everyone else had gone.

'Hello?' she called.

There was no reply.

Desperate not to be left behind, Red started running as fast as she could. Suddenly her foot slipped on a stone and she skidded towards the edge of the path. For a moment her arms spun wildly, before she completely lost her balance and went tumbling down to the valley below.

'. . . Aaarggggghhhhh aaarggggghhhhh aaarggggghhhhh!' yelled Red. She'd been yelling for quite some time now. The world seemed to have stopped spinning though, so she stopped screaming and opened one eye.

She squinted up at a man with more than his fair share of battle scars, less than his fair share of teeth, and half the usual number of eyes.

'You all right?' asked the

man gruffly. 'I thought you was never going to stop screaming!'

'Well, I did just fall down a cliff!' replied Red. 'Or at least –' she squinted up at the path – 'down a really steep hill. I bet *you'd* have screamed too!'

'Not me, missy. I'm a huntsman, see. All that screaming sort of thing is drilled out of you at Huntsmen's College – can't go around being all soft when you do this job.'

'No, I suppose not . . .' said Red cautiously. Everyone knew that in Tale Town, huntsmen *had* to do all sorts of horrible things, usually for the most wicked of wicked witches. It was just the way it had always been.

'So, er, what are you doing here?'

Red asked, trying to sound casual. 'Not, you know, looking for people to kidnap or anything?'

The huntsman grinned. 'Goodness me, no! Well, not right now — it's my lunch break. I was just having a picnic. At least, I was till *you* showed up!' He tugged at the corner of a pretty gingham blanket that Red was sprawled on top of, covered in crumpled paper plates and squashed sandwiches.

'Oh, right . . . sorry about that,' said Red.

'Can't be helped,' the huntsman said. He looked up at the path that Red had just tumbled down from. 'There's a quicker way up to Squirrel-Nose Mountain from down here, if that's

where you're heading,' he added. 'Want me to show you the way?'

Red mulled this over. On the one hand this man was a stranger *and* a huntsman, which meant that he *almost certainly* worked for a wicked witch. On the other hand, he was on his lunch break, and she *did* need to find her friends as quickly as possible.

'OK,' she replied, and after helping the huntsman to pack up his squashed sandwiches, they set off.

'So . . . what brings you to this here island?' asked the huntsman.

'It's kind of a funny story,' said Red. 'You see, me and my friends are meeting a troll at the bottom of the mountain.'

'A *troll*?' replied the huntsman eagerly. 'Not many of them on Squirrel-Nose Island – and *I* should know!'

'Oh? And why's that?'

'Um . . . no reason,' replied the huntsman quickly.

There was a long silence.

'So . . . you like picnics?' asked Red, changing the subject.

'Only in the woods,' replied the huntsman, 'I *love* woods, forests, thickets, coppices, dingles . . . well, trees in general. See, I always wanted to be a woodsman when I was a kid.'

'My dad's a woodsman!' said Red proudly. 'There's *nothing* that he can't do with a felled tree. Cupboards, benches, you name it, he makes it – although his wooden balloons weren't all that great, and sometimes it *would* be nice to shower in water rather than wood chippings . . .'

The huntsman smiled at her. 'Best job in the world!' he replied, going all misty-eyed. 'None of this "*collectin' hearts in boxes*", or "*lockin' up all the girls what's prettier than the wicked witch*", like I have to do! But I don't have any choice.' He paused for a moment, looking incredibly sad.

'Why not?' asked Red.

'Well, there was just one place at the local woodcutting school when I was little, and my brother, well, he cut down his first tree aged three and carved it into a boat by the time he was four – so of course, *he* got the place. And *I* got packed off to Huntsmen's College.'

'That's *so* sad!' said Red. 'But surely, you don't *have* to be a huntsman, there must be lots of other jobs you could do?'

'P'raps,' replied the huntsman thoughtfully. 'I always liked the idea of dragon conversation.'

'Don't you mean "*conservation*"?' asked Red. 'As in, looking after dragons?'

The huntsman shook his head. 'Nah.

I mean "conversation". You know, helping dragons get better at small talk. Chatting to folk at parties, that sort of thing. Poor souls. Everyone thinks they're all confident just because they can breathe fire. But it's tough being all big and scary-looking, nobody gives you the time of day . . .' He sighed heavily, then glanced down at his watch. 'Crikey! Lunch is almost over — you'd best get going. I ain't allowed to be nice while I'm on duty. Truth be told, I don't think I'm *ever* meant to be nice. So come on, get a move on — just up that way and on your left.'

Red scrambled up on to the path. She turned to thank the huntsman — but he'd vanished.

4

Together Again?

Red ran along the path, calling her friends. It wasn't long before she heard an answering shout.

'Red!' yelled Jack. 'Are you OK? We've been looking everywhere for you.'

'Thank *goodness* you're back!' said Rapunzel.

Anansi swung down from the treetops on a rope made of spider silk. He pulled

Red into a tight hug. 'It's OK!' he yelled up into the trees. 'She's safe!'

Red looked up into the canopy where a horde of spiders nodded at Anansi, then scuttled away.

'Can you speak to *any* spider *anywhere*?' she asked.

'Pretty much,' said Anansi. 'Apart from Spanish ones. I've never got the hang of Spanish. Anyway, my mum will be waiting. Red, are you all right to keep going?'

'Of course I am!' said Red. 'I only fell down a cliff!'

They ran on up the path until it stopped at a deep chasm with a couple of frayed ropes dangling from it. The edge of the forest was just on the other side.

'Oh no!' exclaimed Anansi. 'The bridge is down.'

'Down it fell. It fell away! And on this side you'll have to stay!' chanted a high-pitched voice. *'I cut the bridge down with my knife, and that fall now could cost your life!'*

Rapunzel groaned. 'Oh no, it's Rumplestiltskin!'

'Whaaat!' squawked Betsy.

'Seriously?' said Jack. 'That guy is *SO* annoying!'

'Your quest will now end here in vain, if you cannot just guess my name. I'll weave a bridge made out of gold, but first my name has to be told!'

The owner of the voice leaped out from behind a rock, cackling gleefully.

Rapunzel glared at the bearded little man. 'Your name is *Rumplestiltskin!*' she said crossly. 'We *all* know your name. *Everybody* knows your name – it's a pretty hard name to forget! Can you just get on with it and weave us that bridge? We're in a bit of a hurry.'

'It was worth a try . . .' muttered Rumplestiltskin as he pulled out a portable spinning wheel. 'Can you pass me some straw?'

Rapunzel sighed as she gathered up hay from a pile by the side of the path, which the small man spun into gleaming rope. Finally the golden bridge was complete. Rapunzel, Jack and Anansi ran across without a backwards glance, but Red slowed down as she passed Rumplestiltskin.

'Maybe you could think about

changing your name?' she suggested.
'Or coming up with a new riddle?'
Then with a wave she ran on to catch
up with her friends.

'There! Up ahead!' shouted Anansi,
pointing to where the path left the
forest and joined a wide road at the
bottom of the mountain.

Peering out from behind a large rock was an even larger figure – a troll.

'Mum!' called Anansi.

Cautiously his mother came out from behind her rock, a broad smile on her face.

Nobody noticed the thick net dangling from a ledge on the mountain above. Suddenly the net tumbled down, knocking Anansi's mother off her feet. She roared in anger, but before she had time to get free, the net was pulled shut, trapping her.

'Over there!' shouted Jack, pointing to a winch being wound in by a burly man wearing a huntsman's leather cap.

'We need to cut the rope!' yelled Anansi, but before he could get close, the huntsman heaved the troll into a cage on the back of his horse-drawn wagon.

'MUM!' screamed Anansi, as the huntsman's horses started to gallop away. '*Mum . . .*'

———— ◆ ————

'It's not your fault, Red,' said Anansi for at least the twelfth time. 'There's no way you could have known what would happen.'

WHIRRRRRRRrrr...

'You said it yourself, just this morning – I'm too trusting!' replied Red. 'I told that huntsman what we were doing here, and now your mum's gone, and it's *all my fault!*' She gritted her teeth and tried not to cry.

They were standing at a crossroads. The hoofprints and wagon tracks had vanished and they had no idea which way to go next.

Rapunzel, Jack and Anansi were trying to make Red feel better while Betsy was pecking and scratching at the forest floor.

'Come on, Betsy!' said Jack. 'This is no time for eating.'

'Whaaaat?' squawked Betsy angrily.

'What do you mean, you're not eating?'

'WHAAAAAT!'

'Well,' said Jack in surprise. 'I didn't know you could track people! Can hens even smell?'

'Whaaat...' Betsy rolled her eyes.

'Well, it's just that you don't even have a nose!'

'WHAaAT?' shrieked Betsy, sounding very cross.

'OK, OK!' replied Jack, holding his hands up defensively. 'You have an excellent sense of smell and beaks are *way* better than noses. Happy now?'

Suddenly Betsy stood completely still. She scratched at the floor one last time – then shot off like a feathery arrow.

'Come on!' yelled Jack as he sprinted after her. 'Betsy's found something!'

◆ ● ◆

The sun hung low in the sky when the forest suddenly ended and they arrived at a locked gate set into a tall stone wall. Carved skulls and gargoyles peered down at them and a sign warned people to **KEEP OUT OR <u>ELSE!</u>**

Underneath in smaller letters it read: **GUARD DRAGONS PATROL THIS SITE.**

Red glanced at her friends nervously.

'Oh, *come on!*' said Rapunzel. 'People write that sort of thing all the time – it's never actually *true!* Now, how do we get in?'

Everyone was looking at Rapunzel.

She stared blankly back at them for a moment before she understood. 'You want to climb over the wall using my hair?'

Jack looked at her and shrugged. 'Well, if you don't *mind*?'

'I just *had* to ask, didn't I?' Rapunzel muttered as she unwound her hair from its long plaits. The golden strands waved and curled as if they had a life of their own. She threw her hair up and it whipped around one of the scary-looking gargoyles, tying itself into a neat little bow. One by one, they all climbed up Rapunzel's hair and waited for her on the top of the wall.

'You owe me three bottles of conditioner!' Rapunzel complained as she pulled herself up and her hair magically untied itself. Nobody replied — they were all staring silently ahead.

Within the wall, *nothing* was alive. The trees were twisted and dead, and the ground was bare, dry earth. A gleaming road led towards a huge castle in the distance. Rapunzel looked at the road more closely and realized it was made of bones. From inside the castle walls they could hear the unmistakable roar of a dragon.

'Oh . . .' Rapunzel said quietly. 'I guess the sign was serious.'

5

Intruders!

Getting inside the grounds had been easy enough, but getting into the actual castle was *not*.

First, Red had tried knocking on the door. A ghostly figure had appeared and told them that all uninvited visitors were 'encouraged to bear in mind that any attempt to enter the castle would result in a long and incredibly horrible death'. Deciding it was just a trick to scare off visitors, Jack went to try the doorknob. The ghost had reappeared, but this time it skipped most of the message and just repeated '**DEATH**' in a very loud and very creepy voice until they all backed away.

Next Rapunzel had tried to use her hair to reach an open window, but as soon as her golden curls had touched the castle wall, her hair became a huge tangled knot. While Red and Jack were helping Rapunzel to unpick it, nobody noticed a single magic bean drop out of Jack's pocket and burrow into the dry earth.

Finally, Anansi tried to climb a waterspout with the help of some spiders. At first it had seemed as if it was working, but suddenly a torrent of rainwater gushed down, flushing Anansi and all his incy-wincy friends off the wall before soaking into the dry ground around them.

'It's useless!' exclaimed Jack as he helped Anansi up. 'We'll never get in!'

Betsy pointed a wing into the air behind him and squawked,

'WHAAAAAT!?!'

Jack, Red, Rapunzel and Anansi spun around. Thundering up from the now wet earth was a huge, curling beanstalk. It twisted as it grew, thick leaves bursting out either side like rungs on a ladder.

'I was saving that,' said Jack quietly. 'I've hardly got any left.'

'But Jack, *that's* our way in!' exclaimed Red. 'Come on, everyone, *up*!'

Jack stuffed Betsy inside his jumper and everybody scrambled up the beanstalk with Red at the back. She had just passed a window when she heard a voice that she recognized — it was the huntsman! She climbed silently back down to peer in.

'But it looked like a troll!' protested the huntsman. 'You know, big and green an' that.'

'Yes, yes . . .' hissed an impatient voice. 'But it *isn't* a troll, is it?'

Red craned her neck as far as she dared to see who the huntsman was talking to. When she saw, a shiver ran down her spine — it *was* a wicked witch, no doubt about that. Red wasn't sure exactly *how* wicked this one was, but judging by the necklace of skulls that she wore, the answer was probably '*very*'.

'The enchantment isn't even very strong!' continued the witch. 'Why, even my magical necklace would be able to break it!'

A thrill of excitement ran through Red: so there *was* a cure for Anansi's family!

'Do you want me to try and find another troll?' asked the huntsman.

'Of course not!' exclaimed the witch. 'It took you long enough to find this one in the first place. It might not be a "real" troll, but it *looks* like one. *Finally* my collection of magical creatures is complete! Soon I will have my own private magical army!' The witch cackled for a moment, glaring at the huntsman until he half-heartedly joined in.

'Oh, never mind!' she snapped a second later. 'The moment's passed.' She turned on her heel and marched out.

The huntsman's shoulders slumped and Red saw him sigh deeply.

A sudden movement in the corner of the room caught Red's eye. Darting out from behind a tapestry was a girl – a very grubby girl – dressed only in rags. She paused for a second, looking straight at Red, and gestured something that could only mean '*Get out of here*'.

At the exact same moment the witch

burst back into the room. 'Intruders!' she screeched. 'Climbing a beanstalk! I saw them in my crystal ball!'

'Do you mean that great big beanstalk what's growing up outside the window?' asked the huntsman.

'*Of course I do!*' shrieked the witch. 'What *other* beanstalk would it be?'

'Yes, ma'am. Right, ma'am. I'll deal with it!'

'I *wish* I could believe you!' spat the witch.

'But *I* don't think you could deal a pack of cards! So instead let's . . .' She paused dramatically, then screamed, '*RELEASE THE DRAGON!* Mwa-ha, ha, ha, ha, ha, ha!'

The huntsman's shoulders slumped even further as he joined in with the witch's evil laughter. Then he went to do as he was commanded.

———◆———

Red scrambled up the beanstalk as quickly as she could, past thatched roofs and towards the battlements on top of the main tower. It was a long climb and soon she was out of breath. Eventually she could see her friends up above.

'What took *you* so long?' shouted Jack.

'Dragon!' gasped Red breathlessly.

'What?' yelled Jack. 'Flagon? Flagon of what?'

'There's a *dragon*!' repeated Red as she gasped for air.

'There's a wagon?' replied Jack, sounding confused.

Red didn't get the chance to say anything else. There was a ferocious roar, and suddenly Jack, Anansi, Rapunzel and Betsy were all staring down at a huge dragon with a heavy chain wrapped around one leg. It sniffed the air and then flew straight towards them, sparks flying from its mouth.

Red could only cling on to the beanstalk and watch in horror as a huge, clawed foot snatched up her friends as if they were a handful of sweets. The dragon turned in the air, smacking into the beanstalk and sending Red flying. Before she could take a breath, Red landed on a roof and slid down until she was hanging on to a length of guttering. She could see Rapunzel's knotty hair trailing behind the dragon's foot as the creature slowly circled the tower.

Red's mind worked furiously. If she stayed where she was, the dragon would *definitely* see her — but where could she go? She peered down between her dangling legs to the thatched roofs below. Perhaps they would be a soft landing? *Hopefully* . . .

Red took a deep breath, closed her eyes and dropped soundlessly through the air.

6

The Magic Bum

ed crashed through the thatched roof. She'd bounced off one, rolled down another and things had been looking up . . . until this last one gave way beneath her.

Instead of dropping silently, Red was now screaming as loud as she could as she fell towards the flagstones below. 'Gaaaaaaaaaaaaaaaaah!'

There was a puff of smoke and instead

of slamming on to a cold hard floor, Red found herself landing on something surprisingly soft and warm. The flesh-coloured cushion wobbled beneath her as she sat up and looked around.

What was this thing? And where had it come from?

Suddenly she heard high-pitched, uncontrollable laughter. Hovering in the air nearby was a bright blue, almost see-through young boy.

'That is the funniest thing *EVER*!' he squealed.

'*What* is?' demanded Red, feeling annoyed. She'd just fallen through a roof, she had rotten straw poking out of her hair, and *now* she was being laughed at.

'Look what you landed on!' continued the boy. 'It's a bum! I magicked a bum! AMAZING!'

Red looked down. He was right – she was indeed sitting on top of a giant bum.

She tried to wriggle off, but it melted away into nothing.

'You smell of bum! You smell of bum!' sang the boy happily as he whirled around through the air.

'That's *enough*, Cole!' rang out an exasperated voice. Standing in the corner of the room was the same tattered girl that Red had seen in the witch's chambers.

'Sorry about him.' The

girl sighed. 'That's Cole, my Fairy Godbrother. I apologize in advance for anything annoying or horrible that he says . . . or does.'

The Fairy Godbrother responded by looking curiously at Red, then slowly and thoroughly picking his nose.

'You're *disgusting*!' said the girl.

'That's *MEAN*!' shouted the boy. 'You're *always* bossing me!'

He blinked out of sight, leaving Red and the girl alone in the cold dark room.

The girl shrugged. 'He never stays cross for long,' she explained. 'I'm Ella, by the way – it's short for *Cinderella*, but that's a pretty *out there* kind of name so I just stick with Ella.'

'I'm Red.'

'Oh. Er, right,' replied Ella. 'Well, there's nothing wrong with creative names! I mean . . . wouldn't it be boring if we were all called Sally or something!' She paused and looked at Red. 'Your middle name's *not* Sally, is it?'

Red smiled and shook her head.

'Thank goodness!' said Ella. 'So anyway, welcome to our humble home. It was nice of you to drop in.' She looked up to the hole in the thatched roof and grinned.

Red laughed.

'It looks like the dragon didn't see you,' continued Ella. 'She's going a bit blind in one eye, poor thing.'

'*Poor thing?*' exclaimed Red.

'She's a prisoner of the witch too!'

said Ella. 'We all are. I haven't been able to leave the castle in *ages*. Anyway, I know that she's up to *something* — for the past few months she's been sending Wilf out to hunt down magical creatures.'

'Who's Wilf?' asked Red.

'The huntsman,' explained Ella. 'Nice bloke, quite chatty, very big, a bit smelly, you know?'

'I know . . .' replied Red, narrowing her eyes. '*He* kidnapped my friend's mum, and now *I'm* all on my own and

I've got to rescue *everyone*. But I've got no idea where they are – it's going to be *impossible*.' Red tried to blink away the tears that threatened to tumble down her cheeks.

Ella placed an arm over her shoulders. 'Well, most of that might be true,' she said gently. 'Apart from *one* thing . . .'

'What's that?' asked Red sadly.

'You're *not* on your own!' Ella smiled. 'Plus, I'm pretty sure your friends aren't in the dungeons. I heard the witch moaning that the dungeons were already full. So we know we don't have to look in there.'

She looked away from Red and called out, 'Hey! Cole! Fancy playing some tricks on the guards? You can be as silly as you like, I promise I won't shout.'

'Promise?' asked Cole's voice from thin air.

'Promise!' replied Ella. There was a crackle of magical smoke and the room filled with blue light as Cole reappeared.

'You won't be cross if I get things wrong?' he asked.

'Of course not!' said Ella.

'Even if I make it rain rabbit poo instead of unlocking a door, or something like that?'

'*Even* if you do that,' said Ella. 'Listen, Cole, I'm sorry I shouted at you earlier – I didn't mean it.'

'That's all right!' exclaimed Cole happily. 'I'd forgotten anyway. So . . . who are we rescuing?'

Red smiled. Suddenly, the world seemed a little bit brighter.

'But *gosh*! Just look at the state of me!' gasped Ella, looking down at her ragged clothing. 'I can't meet your friends like this! I *have* to get changed!' She hurried off into the next room.

Cole had one finger stuck firmly up his nose when he looked over at Red.

'Sorry!' he mumbled, removing his

finger and wiping it on his trousers.

Red grinned at him. 'Do you want to know a secret?' she whispered.

The Fairy Godbrother's eyes lit up and he nodded.

'Sometimes I pick my nose too!'

Cole's eyes grew wide with delight.

'But you mustn't tell *anyone!*' continued Red. 'Especially my friend Rapunzel. She'd think it was *gross!*'

Cole nodded, suddenly serious. 'Of course not!' he said solemnly. 'A secret's a secret!'

He paused for a moment. 'Do you want to know *my* secret?' he asked.

Red nodded.

'I think my magic's broken,' said Cole. 'All of the other fairies tease me – none of my spells ever come out right, and they never last very long either.'

'I'm sure you'll get better at it when you're a bit bigger . . .' said Red.

'Maybe,' said Cole sadly. 'Promise you won't tell Ella! I'm her Fairy Godbrother . . .' He sniffed loudly. 'If *she* knew my magic was broken she'd swap me for a better one!'

He looked so upset that Red ran over and gave him a hug. 'Come on, Cole, cheer up! Ella would *never* do that!'

'What are you two whispering

about?' asked Ella as she walked back into the room. Cole stared at Red in a *'You promised!'* sort of way.

'Oh, nothing . . .' said Red casually. *'Wow!* I love that dress!'

'Thank you!' beamed Ella. She patted down the collection of rags she was wearing. They looked even dirtier than the clothes she had just changed out of.

'This is my *very best* dress, for special occasions!' Ella swept her hair back elegantly, leaving a grimy smudge across her face.

'Very nice!' said Red with a slight grin. 'So . . . how do we get out of here?'

7

Room without a View

*J*ack, Anansi and Rapunzel sat on the floor in a completely bare room with one heavily barred window high above and a securely locked door. Betsy had scrambled up to the windowsill and was peering sadly out.

When the dragon had first dumped them on the floor of the courtyard, Jack had been *so* relieved to still be alive. He had felt a renewed passion for life and promised that he would make the most of every single moment from then on.

That was before the guards had collected them and marched them up to this completely empty cell at the top of the tower. Now Jack was worried that he might die of boredom instead.

'What do you think Red's doing?' he asked. 'I hope she's OK.'

'That must be the *bazillionth* time you've asked that!' said Rapunzel. 'As I've said every other time, *I've got no idea*, and *Yes, me too.*'

'Oh,' said Jack. 'Sorry. I'm just a bit bored. Hey! Shall we play a game? Yeah! Come on, guys! Hmmm, how about . . . I-spy?'

Rapunzel rolled her eyes and Anansi

seemed to be grinding his teeth. Even Betsy was scowling.

'I spy, with my little eye, something beginning with . . .' Jack looked around the empty room. 'W!'

'Walls,' said Rapunzel without even looking up. Jack sighed and they all fell silent again. Moments later there was a quiet hiss behind the door.

'Probably just those guards again,' said Jack.

But he was wrong.

Coils of foul-smelling smoke drifted under the door and gathered in the middle of the room. They danced in a dizzying whirl until they had taken the shape of a person. Then the smoke vanished, leaving in its place a *very* wicked-looking witch.

Rapunzel stood up furiously. 'You can't keep us here! I'm a *princess*! When my father hears about—'

The witch clicked her fingers and Rapunzel's voice vanished – she opened and shut her mouth furiously, but no sound came out at all.

'Nobody will hear *anything* from *you* for a while,' the witch said. 'Now, what on *EARTH* would possess you to think that you, a group of *children* –' she spat the last word as if it were poisonous – 'could break into *my* castle?'

'You've got my mum,' said Anansi. 'You kidnapped her!'

'And what would I want with your mum?' sneered the witch. 'Does she have powerful magic? Is she extremely rare or precious?'

'Yes!' replied Anansi glaring at her.

The witch's eyes lit up. 'Really?' she asked. 'How?'

'She's my *mum*,' replied Anansi.

The witch sighed. 'Well, this is all *terribly* sentimental, but I can assure you, your mother isn't here.'

'You're lying!' shouted Anansi. 'We followed the huntsman's trail, right to this castle!'

'Ahh!' said the witch, a smile creasing her face unpleasantly. 'I *see*!' She began to laugh. 'The troll? Am I right? Oh, well that's just *splendid*!'

'So . . . will you let her go?' asked Anansi.

'*Of course not!*' snorted the witch. 'But it's good to have that mystery cleared up.' She was about to say something else when a buzzing noise came out of her pocket, getting louder by the second. The witch reached into her gown and pulled out a glowing crystal ball, which she inspected closely. At first her mouth curled angrily, then it lifted at the corners and stretched into a cruel smile.

'Well, that'll save me a job!' she said with an evil cackle.

'What will?' asked Anansi.

'Now *that* is none of your business!' replied the witch. She laughed one more horrible laugh, turned back into smoke and drifted away through the cracks around the door.

'**Whaaat!**' said Betsy after a moment's silence.

'I know,' agreed Jack. 'She wasn't very nice *at all*. Even so, there's no need to use bad language!'

8

Back to the Fewchur

Red crept along a tiny passageway behind Ella, with Cole's faint glow leading the way. Thick curtains of spider webs brushed her and she could feel scurrying shapes dart past in the darkness.

'It's *such* a mess down here!' whispered Ella. 'These tunnels really could do with a spring clean!'

'You don't say,' muttered Red as

something cold, wet and slimy stuck to the side of her face. She grimaced as she pulled it off and tossed it behind her.

'Still, they're the only way I can get around the castle without the witch knowing,' continued Ella. 'Now, wait a second, I'll just check the room's empty, then we can sneak out and search the rest of the floor.' Everything went silent for a moment, then Ella whispered, 'Come on, the coast's clear!' Red moved forward and tumbled into a creepy-looking chamber. Animal skeletons, spikes and season.

Ella and Red tiptoed towards the door, but they could hear two guards having an argument on the other side.

'*Try it. You'll love it!*'

'*It's just a banana with some almonds stuck in. It's not a new food.*'

'*It is! I've called it an Alm-ana.*'

'*That's ridiculous!*'

'*What foods have you ever invented?*'

'*Loads!*'

'*Like what?*'

'*Well, one time I took a handful of almonds and poked them into a banana. I called it a Ban-almond.*'

'*That sounds horrible!*'

'It was really tasty, actually! Far nicer than your stupid Alm-ana.'

Red looked over at Ella. 'We don't have time for this!' she whispered.

Ella nodded. 'Cole, can you get rid of those guards?'

'Let's see . . .' said Cole thoughtfully. He started a wild dance, spinning through the air until he was just a glowing blur. Suddenly he stopped in a bizarre pose, his face a mask of intense concentration. He clicked his fingers three times and muttered some magic words.

Outside the door Red heard two loud shrieks.

'My hair! It's falling out!'

'*My beard won't stop growing!*'

There was the muffled sound of two men running away through a sea of beard hair, then silence.

Slowly Ella inched the door open and peered out. 'It worked!' she said.

'They're gone! Good work, Cole!'

'It's not as easy as it looks, you know!' replied Cole, then leaned in and whispered to Red, 'I was *trying* to turn them into statues!'

* ◆ *

Red, Ella and Cole had explored countless rooms on the castle's many floors and had so far rescued *none* of Red's friends. They *had* however stopped in each room so that Ella could sweep out a fireplace or do some dusting, and in one instance scrub the whole floor.

They were creeping down a long, winding corridor when Red suddenly shrieked, '*Ouch!* Something bit me!'

'Sorry!' muttered Ella.

'You bit me?' gasped Red.

'It was a needle,' explained Ella. 'There's a hole in your hood, so I thought I'd patch it up.'

'While we're in the middle of a rescue mission?' cried Red.

'Of course!' replied Ella. 'Or it might get even bigger!'

'Look, Ella, you've got to stop all the tidying!' snapped Red. 'We don't have . . .' She stopped when she noticed Cole waving frantically at them both.

'*Guards!*' he whispered.

Red froze. The corridor had no doorways, no windows, no *nothing* – there was nowhere to hide.

'*Just keep cutting it!*' said a voice from the bend behind them.

'*I do,*' replied another. '*But it keeps growing back.*'

'*I KNOW,*' said the first voice. '*It keeps tripping me up. That's why you need to keep cutting it!*'

'*You're just jealous of my beard because you've gone bald!*'

'*I'm not jealous!*' said the first voice. '*I just don't know why the boss won't reverse the spell – she's so mean!*'

'*Of course she's mean!*' snapped the second voice. '*She's a wicked witch!*'

'Cole!' hissed Ella. 'Do something. *Anything!*'

The Fairy Godbrother thought for a moment, then he leaped into the air and performed another chaotic dance. There was a puff of smoke and a door appeared in the wall next to them. On it hung a hastily painted sign reading:

to the fewchur

'Where's "*the fewchur*"?' whispered Red.

'No idea!' replied Ella. 'But it's either there or the guards take us to the dungeons!' She opened the door and they all leaped through.

Red was extremely surprised to discover that the door led back to *exactly* where they had just come from − except the guards were no longer behind them, they were *just* in front. Red held her breath and tried to be as quiet as possible.

The smaller guard was completely bald and carrying a plate piled with mouldy bread. The bigger guard held a large pair of shears, which he used every few seconds to chop off his fast-growing beard.

'*Why'd she have to put those kids in the highest room in the tower?*' grumbled the bald guard as they walked away. '*Why not down in the dungeon with that troll and the rest of 'em? I'll bet it was just so that we have to keep going* up and down to take 'em their food. *You know, just to make us that little bit more miserable . . . I'm starting to think she really hates me . . .'*

'*She's not the only one,*' muttered the bearded guard as they disappeared around a bend.

'That's the furthest I've *EVER* been able to go!' whispered Cole excitedly, 'Eight WHOLE seconds into the future! AMAZING!'

Red smiled as she realized what '*To the fewchur*' meant. 'Well done, Cole!' she said, ruffling his blue hair. 'And *now* we know where my friends are too.'

9
A Daring Escape

*J*ack looked around the room. There had to be *something* that he'd missed — *something* he hadn't noticed yet . . . It couldn't end like this! Then he saw it — a tiny screw, dug into the cement around the door frame — and his face lit up. This was *it*: just what he needed!

Jack grinned. 'I spy, with my little—'

'*NO!*' yelled Anansi. 'No more, Jack! *Please* no more. It's either: wall, floor, floorboard, brick, nail, door, doorway, window or cement. We've been playing I-spy for *FIVE HOURS* now and I. Can't. Take it. *ANY MORE!*'

'It wasn't any of those things, *actually*,' Jack muttered. 'It was "screw".'

A sudden squeak beneath his feet distracted him. He looked down at the wooden floor which had suddenly started shaking.

'Do you think it's the witch again?' asked Jack.

Rapunzel shrugged and started trying to mime that she really needed to get her voice back, but to Jack it just looked like she was pretending to eat a bowl of imaginary spaghetti.

'Sorry?' said Jack. 'What was that?'

Rapunzel's shoulders slumped as the floor shook again, more powerfully this time.

Everyone leaped back as an explosion of floorboards shot up in a cloud of dust, followed by a glowing, see-though boy! '**Whaaaat?**' screeched Betsy.

'I don't know!' replied Jack. Then he looked down at the hole in the floor – there was someone else down there! '*Red!*' he yelled, running forward to help her up. 'You're all right!'

'Of course!' said Red, grinning. 'I only got chased by a dragon, fell through a roof, narrowly avoided DEATH, travelled to the future and escaped the guards. It's just as well, really, otherwise you'd *never* be getting out of here!'

She turned to help pull Ella up too.

'But what happened?' asked Anansi. 'Who's this? How did you find us?'

'Well, that's all thanks to Ella and Cole,' replied Red, pointing at her two new friends. 'Ella's got a network of secret tunnels that lead all through the castle. And not only that – we know where your mum is!'

'What?' exclaimed Anansi. 'How?'

'There's no time right now!' said Red. 'We've got to get out of here!'

There was the sound of someone frantically jumping up and down and clapping their hands together.

'Why are you doing *that*?' Red asked Rapunzel.

'She lost her voice,' whispered Jack. 'Well, I guess it was more stolen, but still, you know . . .'

Rapunzel glared at Jack, then took a deep breath and wrote a message in the dust on the floor: 'Seriously? You expect me to crawl through that filthy tunnel?'

'Ah . . . you must be Rapunzel?' said Cole, with a quick smile at Red. 'I've heard all about you. Well, don't worry, I can cast a spell that means no dirt will touch you – *and* you'll get your voice back!'

'You can do magic?' said Jack eagerly.

'Ahem . . . well, sort of . . .' fumbled Cole, before beginning again. 'I mean, *yeah*, of course!'

'Cool!' said Anansi and Jack.

'OK, well, do your thing, Cole,' replied Ella. 'But be quick, the witch doesn't know we're here – *yet* – but it's only a matter of time.'

———— ◆◆ ————

'It is *not* funny,' snapped Rapunzel, glaring at Cole as they crawled down the dusty tunnel.

'It is a *bit* funny,' said Jack quietly.

'It is *not*,' repeated Rapunzel firmly. Above her, a small cloud produced a steady rain of rabbit droppings.

'I'm with Rapunzel,' muttered Anansi from behind her. 'These rabbit poos are everywhere – I keep squashing my hands into them!'

'It was an accident!' protested Cole. 'Ella was hurrying me along and . . . well, I got it wrong . . . I'm sorry.' His voice brightened. 'Hopefully it won't last *too* much longer – and at least you got your voice back.'

'I suppose,' said Rapunzel with a sigh. 'So how much longer do we have to crawl along this *filthy* tunnel?'

'Not much,' said Ella. 'Everyone, be quiet – we're getting near the exit.'

They crawled on; the only sound was the gentle pitter-patter of rabbit poo falling on Rapunzel's head.

At the end, Ella peered out to check for guards. Then, one by one, they shuffled out of the tunnel, rubbing their sore knees and, in Anansi's case, wiping his hands on his trousers.

'This way . . .' whispered Ella, leading the group to a narrow staircase. 'The

dungeons are in the very bottom of the castle, and *this* is the only way down.'

———◆———

As they walked through the maze of corridors that made up the dungeons, Red shuddered; there was something so cold and horrible about this place, plus it smelt bad – *really* bad.

All the doors they passed were locked, but when they peered in, every cell was empty.

'So . . . where's my mum?' whispered Anansi.

'I don't know . . .' replied Ella. 'It's weird, isn't it? The witch has been capturing *hundreds* of magical creatures – so where are they all?'

They crept on until they saw a faint

light flickering ahead in the darkness.

'That way, I guess,' whispered Red.

The passageway curled round to the left, so they couldn't see what lay ahead until they found themselves staring into a huge circular chamber at the heart of the dungeons. The stone walls rose up high overhead with a huge central pillar that held up the vaulted ceiling. Chained up in a huge cell opposite them was a troll – Anansi's mother.

'Mum!' Anansi called out,

running towards her. 'Don't worry, we'll get you out!'

'I wouldn't be so sure about *that*!' A cruel voice rang out as the witch appeared inside a glowing ring circling the central pillar. The ring was made up of strange signs and symbols that shifted and danced in the dim light.

The witch muttered a few words under her breath and Red felt the ground tremble as a stone slab crashed down, blocking off the passage they had come through and trapping them in the dungeon. The trembling went on as large sections of the circular wall spun slowly around, revealing hundreds of stone cells, each with a different magical creature chained up inside. There was the dragon that had captured them earlier, a three-headed dog with saliva dripping from its fangs, a golem, a griffin, a hydra, a rather depressed-looking unicorn and many, *many* more.

'Behold!' screeched the witch. 'The

makings of my magical army!'

Then she laughed and laughed and *laughed*, until the echo of her laughter drowned out any other sound.

10

An Evil Scheme

*T*he wicked witch was *still* laughing as Red and the others looked at each other uneasily – she'd been laughing now for well over two minutes.

'Now what?' asked Rapunzel quietly.

'Same as before!' replied Anansi. '*Now* we rescue my mum! Cole, can you use your magic to break her chains and get us all out of here?'

Everyone turned to look at Cole, whose glowing blue ears flushed pink.

'Well, um . . .' muttered Cole. 'The thing is . . .' He sighed heavily and took a deep breath. 'I'll try.' He began to perform his spell dance.

The witch stopped laughing and watched Cole with interest.

Suddenly Cole's whirling stopped and he hung motionless in the air. Surprise rippled across his face, shortly followed by worry, and finally fear.

'*Yeeeaaaaaaaarrrrrrrrrrggggggghhhhhh!*' he yelled as bright blue sparks popped off him in all directions. He burst into the air, leaving a trail of magical smoke behind him. Red, Jack and the others ducked as he shot overhead, bouncing

around the
dungeon like a
piece of exploding
popcorn.
Eventually he
skidded to a halt,
lying dazed on
the dungeon floor,
right next to the
witch.

'I *completely*
forgot to say,'
cackled the witch,
'any magic cast in
this room outside
of the safety of my
magic circle will
backfire! I mean,

really, children — do you take me for a fool?' She tutted. 'How do you think I'm holding all these creatures here?' She gestured at the magical beasts. 'Each one of them would *love* to get their teeth into me — but they're powerless! The only place where magic *is* possible — is here.' She pointed down at the glowing ring on the ground. 'Which is where I shall be taking your little friend.' She clicked her fingers and Cole's slumped figure slid across the flagstones, bumping into the central column.

'No!' screamed Ella, lunging forward. The witch waved her hand vaguely in Ella's direction. Green shoots sprang up from the floor at Ella's feet, thickening into a tangled mass of thorns until she was completely surrounded. Red tried to help, but the spiky prison spread outward until Red, Jack, Betsy, Rapunzel and Anansi were also trapped in their own thorny cells.

Red peered through the prickly branches surrounding her as the witch used her magic to control Cole as though he was a puppet. First she made him stand up, and then she made him do backflips and other clumsy dance moves.

'This *is* fun!' the witch exclaimed.

'Let him go!' shouted Ella.

'I'm afraid I can't do *that*!' replied the witch. 'You see, I need him for my spell.'

'But why?' sobbed Ella. '*Surely* your magic is powerful enough to do anything you want?'

'Well, I'm glad you can see that!' said the witch. 'Most people fail to come close to grasping the depth of my skills — it's all just "*Please don't hurt me*" or "*Arggh, you've turned my arm into a tail*". It's so selfish! I am, as you say, IMMENSELY powerful. *However . . .*' The witch sighed. 'This spell is *supposed* to be for bringing magical creatures back to areas where they have been forgotten about, or died out. So, at its heart it is a "*good*" spell, which means that I, as a *wicked* witch, am not able to cast it.' She paused for a moment. 'But what if a good fairy happened to be at the heart of the spell? What if I used his "*goodness*" to fulfil *my* needs? Why, then I would *finally* have my loyal magical army!' She narrowed her eyes and stared at Ella. 'Why else do you think I first brought you and your fairy creature to stay here? I've been planning

this for a *long* time! And now that I have
a troll, my collection is complete!' She
burst out laughing again – then looked
around with a disappointed expression.
'Huntsman!' she screeched, a stormy
expression on her face. *'Huntsman!'*

Immediately the huntsman bustled
out of the stone cell the dragon
was chained up in.

'Sorry, ma'am,' he muttered. 'The dragon had a nasty splinter in her paw, so I thought I'd just . . .'

The witch traced a finger across her narrow lips and the huntsman fell silent. 'Is there even a *shred* of villainy within you?' she hissed. 'Does any part of you want to even *try* to be evil?'

The huntsman shuffled his feet and looked at the floor. 'I'm sorry, I just . . .'

'Oh *forget* it!' shouted the witch. 'Chain that fairy up here —' she gestured to a hollow in the central column — 'and we can get on, unless you're worried that *he* might have a splinter too?'

'No, ma'am — will do, ma'am,' said the huntsman, walking forward to gently pick Cole up. 'Come on, little fella,' he whispered under his breath. 'Up you get . . .'

Seconds later Cole was securely fixed to the huge central column.

The witch grinned. '*Now* it is time!' she cried with an evil laugh, flinging her arms up and holding them trembling in the air for a second. There was a devastating *CRACK*, as though the entire world had just split open, and the room filled with smoke and a dazzling blue light.

Through the confusion Red could see Cole slump down further against the magical chains that held him, his head heavy on his chest.

'Cole!' screamed Ella. '*Cole!*'

All they could do was watch as brightly coloured streams of magic rose out of Cole in a twisting spiral. The ribbons of magic darkened as they flowed across the ceiling in rivers of churning smoke, winding towards the cells packed with magical creatures, like snakes stalking their prey.

11

The Turncoat

A terrifying sound filled the chamber. Red could see all the magical creatures shivering and shuddering as the magic reached them. The dragon tried to flex its wings, desperate for escape, but the chains and enchantments holding it were too strong.

The more Red looked at the dragon, the harder it became to see. It was as if there were two dragons, somehow overlapping each other. With a ghastly ripping sound, the 'new' dragon peeled itself away and stood shimmering in the dim light. It was almost completely see-through, as though it wasn't *really* there at all.

The witch raised her hand and the newly born dragon strode out of the cell towards her. '*Look!*' she screeched at the huntsman. 'It's working!'

The huntsman looked at the ghostly creatures filling up the dungeon and tried his best to look pleased.

'Er, yeah! With all them magical beasts you'll be able to be right nasty to *loads* of people.' He paused for a moment, before slowly adding, 'Huh-huh-huh-haaar . . .'

'That was a *pathetic* attempt at being evil,' replied the witch. 'But I appreciate the effort.'

———— ◆ ◆ ————

Red put her head in her hands. This was all *her* fault! Anansi had got it right back in Tale Town – she *was* too trusting!

'Never,' she sobbed bitterly, '*never* again . . .'

'*What?*' shouted Ella from the cell next to her.

'This is all *my* fault!' spat Red. 'It's because I trusted that huntsman – I told him we were meeting a troll. I'll never trust *anyone* again!'

Ella's face fell. 'Come on, Red, this isn't *your* fault,' she said. 'If it wasn't Anansi's mum, then Wilf would have found a different troll and the witch would *still* be trying to make a magical army. And sure, maybe some people just *aren't* trustworthy, but what are you going to do? Never trust anyone *ever* again? If I'd done that when the witch first captured me, I'd never have met Cole – and you and I would never have become friends! Wouldn't that be awful?'

Red smiled weakly at her friend.

'Thanks, Ella, it's just . . .' She swallowed a sob. 'I'm just so sorry to have got you all trapped down here.'

Ella shrugged. '"*Sorry*" isn't going to save Cole. "*Sorry*" isn't going to save any of us! So, forget about feeling sorry, and let's start thinking of a way out of here! OK?'

Red nodded. Ella was right. There *had* to be a way out of this – there was always *something* . . .

'And one more thing,' added Ella. 'You know Wilf, the huntsman? He's not all bad, so go easy on him, OK?'

Red nodded. Then it hit her. The huntsman! *He* was their ticket out of there. It was clear that he wasn't *really* on the witch's side. If she could just convince him to help them, then *maybe* they'd have a chance?

◆ ◆ ◆

'*Wilf!*' Red shouted through the walls of her thorny prison, '*Wilf!* Over here!'

The huntsman peered over. He glanced at the witch, who was too busy with her new magical beasts to pay him any attention, then crept over cautiously.

'You all right in there, missy?' he whispered.

'Well, that's kind of the thing,' Red replied. 'Not *really* . . . You see, everything would be *loads* better if I wasn't trapped in this cage of thorns. You know, like if me and my friends could *somehow* escape?'

'But the mistress . . .' said Wilf, chewing his lip. 'She wouldn't like that one bit!'

'I guess not,' said Red. 'But you know, Wilf . . . I *can* call you Wilf, can't I?'

The big man nodded and smiled a gappy smile.

'So, Wilf, how about this . . . how about you *stop* working for her? I know that you hate it! You're not a huntsman — not *really* — you're a *woodsman*! You could come and work for my dad. You should see the axes he's got — *hundreds of them!*'

Wilf's eyes lit up. 'Hundreds?' he asked disbelievingly.

'Oh yeah!' Red nodded. 'They're *super*-sharp. All different sorts too!'

Wilf looked torn. He glanced nervously around the room. More and more of the ghostly creatures were filling the dungeon, and Cole was looking paler and paler, his glow slowly going out.

'Yeah,' he said slowly. 'This don't look great, does it? OK. All right then — I'll help. What do you need?'

'Have you got an axe?' Red asked.

Wilf grinned. 'What do *you* think?' He reached one hand behind his back and pulled out a huge, gleaming axe.

'Stand back!' he said, grinning as he heaved the axe back, then swung it round, chopping through the thorny branches as though they were matchsticks.

Seconds later Red was out of her prison and darting for cover. All she had to do *now* was lure the witch out of her magic circle.

12

What's in a Name?

'**I** don't believe it!' the witch screamed. The huntsman's chopping had finally caught her attention. '*Seriously?* You're seriously going to side with *them*? Against . . .' She paused. '*Me?*'

'Nothin' personal, ma'am,' said Wilf. 'But I ain't like you! I've never been wicked – not deep down. And while I'm sayin' all this . . . You know that young lass you told me to take out into the woods and "take care of" last year?'

'Yes?' hissed the witch

'Well I *did* take care of her.'

The witch nodded. 'Glad to hear it.'

'You don't understand,' replied Wilf. 'I'm *still* looking after her. I found her a room at a little cottage, an' there's these seven little fellas that live there with her. Every other Sunday I go over there for lunch.'

The witch glared at him coldly. 'You have *failed* me, huntsman,' she hissed.

'See, that's just it!' said Wilf. 'I'm not *really* a huntsman, not in my heart. In my heart I'm a . . .'

'You're a *what*?' spat the witch.

'. . . I'm a woodsman,' he said, proudly.

'Is that so?' screeched the witch. 'Then you shall have your wish!' She clicked her fingers and Wilf suddenly froze. For a moment he looked surprised, then his skin hardened and darkened, becoming pitted like bark. In less than three seconds it was impossible to tell that the tree which now stood there had ever even been a person.

'No!' screamed Red, stepping out from behind the cages her friends were trapped in. 'How could you?'

'It was quite simple actually,' said the witch. 'I only used a basic shape-shifting spell with a few extra touches – but you're right, to do it with just a click of my fingers *was* rather impressive.'

Red glared at the witch as an idea came to her. 'What *other* things can you do?' she asked. 'I bet you couldn't turn me into a skeleton just by, I don't know . . . tapping me on the nose?'

'Simple!' exclaimed the witch – and almost took a step out of the magical circle towards Red. She looked down at her feet and then looked back at Red with something almost like respect.

'Clever girl!' she muttered, nodding slowly. 'Not quite clever enough, though.'

Red's heart sank. So much for her brilliant plan.

'And *now*, I shall turn you into a skeleton,' continued the witch, grinning a jagged smile from awful ear to awful ear. 'But . . . from over *here*!' She clearly felt this was a good time for a *really* evil cackle and even went so far as to start off with a '*Mwa-ha-ha-haaaaaaa!*'.

Red wasn't listening — she was looking at the witch's magical army.

None of the new creatures had become *fully* solid yet, and the spell seemed to be slowing down. It looked like Cole's fairy magic wasn't strong enough to power the witch's dark spell. Perhaps there still *was* a way out of this, after all?

'Hey!' she shouted, interrupting the witch mid-cackle. 'Hey, you!'

'You dare to address me *thus*?' demanded the witch.

'I guess I do,' said Red.

The witch's mouth gaped, utterly lost for words.

'Anyway . . .' continued Red, 'I've heard there's this wicked witch that's *SO* evil she can turn laughter into snakes. You've heard of her, right?'

The witch frowned and shook her head.

Red pretended to look surprised. 'Really? That's odd – I thought everyone knew about her. She's got the largest magical army this side of Far Far Away! People say that *her* level of wickedness could *never* be matched. They say that *all* the other witches are about as evil as hamsters compared to her.'

The witch's eyes goggled. '*Nonsense!*' she hissed. 'I am *ALL* powerful! This *other* witch will kneel before me!'

'Fair enough,' replied Red. 'But you might need a bigger army.'

'*Huntsman!*' screamed the witch. 'Chain this girl up. I need to . . . *Oh.*' She suddenly remembered that she'd just turned her huntsman into a tree. 'Never mind! I shall create an army the size of which has *NEVER* been seen before!'

She raised her hands high into the air, pulling magic out of Cole at a faster and faster rate. 'The whole world will *TREMBLE* at my approach!' A wind picked up and roared through the dungeon, almost knocking Red from her feet.

'Gaaahhh!' screamed Rapunzel, Anansi, Jack and Ella from inside their cages.

'Whaaat! Whaaaat? WHAAAAAT!?!' clucked Betsy over the din.

'My name will bring *dread* and *fear* to all who hear it!' screamed the witch. 'I will flatten mountains and—'

'What *is* your name anyway?' yelled Red through the wind that rushed past.

'What?' yelled the witch, dropping her hands for a moment. 'My name? It's Shirley – Shirley the *Incredibly* Evil. Now *be quiet*! I'm in the middle of a rant. Where was I? Oh yes! The skies will blacken at my approach, it will always be summer but *never* the summer holidays . . .'

As the witch went on, and on, and *on*, Red watched the magic flowing out of Cole start to sputter and jolt as if it was running out. The ghostly magical creatures in the room flickered in and out of sight.

'I've just got one more question,' shouted Red, interrupting the witch yet again.

The witch rolled her eyes. 'What *now*?'

'If you're so *amazingly* evil, how come I've never heard of you?'

The witch glared at Red with a look of pure fury. 'Soon *everyone* will have heard of *MEEEEEeeeeEEeeEEEee*!' she screamed. She turned to Cole and tried to increase the speed and power of the spell even more.

The dungeon became a throbbing, roaring mass of half-made creatures and wild magic. Sparks flew in all directions as the witch closed her eyes and gritted her teeth, desperately trying to make Cole release more and more magic – until eventually . . .

The spell broke.

The witch's magical army began to fade. Like old balloons, they became wrinkled and soft. Soon all that was left was a collection of faintly glowing shapes where the beasts used to be, and a moment later, even those were gone. Red glanced over to see Cole lifting his head groggily.

The powerful, roaring wind had stopped completely and was replaced by something even more terrifying: silence – and the witch's cold, terrible rage.

'*What have you done?*' she screamed. 'You've ruined *everything*!'

Red took a few steps back towards the edge of the dungeon.

'I'll make you *sorry*!' continued the witch, starting to walk towards Red. 'I shall create an enchantment *SO* strong that it can *never* be broken! And you will not enjoy it *one little bit.*'

The witch was getting closer and closer, her eyes blazing furiously. 'Cursing you will be *easy!*' she hissed. 'Anger is the strongest emotion, and when you combine it with my power – it is *unstoppable!*' She laughed a cruel, bitter laugh, raised her hands high in the air and swept them down towards Red.

Red had no time to think, or say, or do anything. She flung her hands around her head and curled up into a ball.

A furious heat filled the room, along with a light brighter than any Red could have thought possible. A scream rang out, and it took a second for Red to realize that it wasn't coming from her.

She looked up to see the witch's face twisted with horror as she recognized her mistake. She was now outside the magic circle. Swirling lights spun in dizzying circles, getting brighter and brighter with each moment.

'I suppose it's too late to say "*I'm sorry*"?' asked the witch, as the light reached a blinding point of brilliance and flared out across the dungeon with a roar.

The light fell away. Where the witch had been standing was a small sizzling

pile of . . . *something*, surrounded
by the gruesome skull necklace.

As soon as the witch had vanished,
so did her magic.
Wilf turned back
into a normal
person – the kind
who doesn't
grow leaves –
and the prisons of
thorns crumbled
into dust.

Anansi ran over to his mum, who was
slumped against the wall, recovering
from the effects of the magic, while
Red and Ella dashed towards Cole to
check he was all right.

Jack, Rapunzel and Betsy just looked around the dungeon in amazement – it had been quite a day.

'So, what *now*?' asked Rapunzel.

'Same as before.' Anansi grinned as he helped his mother to her feet. 'We've rescued my mum, so now we get out of here!'

'After we've set all this lot free!' added Red, indicating the hundreds of magical beasts that were still chained up. 'Wilf, have you got a set of keys?'

'What makes you think I need *keys*?' The woodsman grinned, brandishing his axe. 'They'll be out of those chains in no time!'

13

The Witch's Last Spell

*C*old air whooshed over Red,
Rapunzel, Anansi and Jack as they
flew above the moonlit clouds. Betsy
was hidden under Jack's jumper, letting
out a quiet 'What' every now and again.
Although Betsy was a bird, it turned
out she had a terrible fear of flying.

Ella, Wilf and Anansi's mother had
come too, and they were *all* sitting
comfortably on the back of the dragon

as it flew over the sea between the mainland and Squirrel-Nose Island. After Wilf had pulled the splinter out of the dragon's foot and set her free, she had been more than happy to fly them all to Tale Town. Cole flew alongside, like a bright blue shooting star.

Red glanced down at the witch's necklace clutched in her hands – she didn't like holding it, but she also *really* didn't want to drop it. After all, the witch had said that the necklace could break the curse on Anansi's family. They just needed to find out *how*.

◆◆◆

Less than half an hour later, the dragon flew down into the woods just south of Tale Town. Rapunzel had pointed out that landing a massive dragon with a troll on its back at night in the middle of town would have raised a few questions, as well as a lot of spears, so they'd decided it was best to stay undercover.

During the journey, Red had asked Cole to fly on ahead and see if he could find Anansi's uncle Rufaro and bring him to meet them. Rufaro had spent the last year trying to work out how to break the curse that had turned him and Anansi's mother into trolls. Perhaps *he* might know what to do with the necklace?

As soon as they were on the ground, everyone slipped off the dragon's broad back, but when Wilf went to climb down, the dragon made such a sad sound that Wilf paused.

'You want me to stay?' he asked quietly.

The dragon started doing something that seemed very much like purring; although she purred so hard that the ground shook and a nearby tree fell over. Dragons don't really do *quiet* purring.

'Looks like Destiny's takin' me elsewhere, missy,' Wilf said to Red with a smile.

'OK,' replied Red. 'But you're welcome to come back any time. I'm sure my dad would be happy to have another woodsman around.'

'Will do,' said Wilf. 'And listen, if you ever need help – just send a message and me and Destiny will be there in a flash. Ain't that right, Destiny?'

The dragon nodded and nuzzled her huge head into Red, knocking her off her feet, before springing into the sky on her powerful legs.

Within seconds she and Wilf were just a tiny dot against the moon, and then they were gone.

Ella looked around the dark forest and said, 'So . . . what now?'

'Now we wait for Rufaro,' said Red. 'And hope that he knows how to use *this* thing!' She held up the necklace, being careful to not touch any of the more horrible-looking things on it.

'How to use *what*?' called a deep voice from the undergrowth.

Cole burst out from the leaves like a blue firework, followed seconds later by Rufaro.

'Ruffy!' shouted Anansi's mum as she rushed forward to hug her brother. There was a booming crash as the two trolls collided.

'Adeola!' exclaimed Rufaro, swinging his sister around and knocking down another tree. 'It's so good to see you!' Then Rufaro caught his nephew's eye. 'Hello there, Anansi. What have you lot been up to now?' He looked at the necklace that Red was holding out and frowned. 'And where did you get *that*?'

'It's a long story . . .' said Red.

'It usually is!' replied Rufaro with a grin. 'Have you any idea what that thing actually is?'

'Well I know that it belonged to a witch — you know, a *properly* wicked one,' said Red. 'And I know that *she* thought it would be powerful enough to break your curse — I heard her say so.'

Rufaro nodded slowly. 'Yes . . . it's full of dark magic,' he said hesitantly. '*Dangerous* magic . . .'

'But would it work?' interrupted Anansi.

'Well . . .' said Rufaro.

'*Well?*'

Rufaro sighed heavily. 'Possibly, yes. But I have no idea what the side effects would be. This sort of magic can all be a bit . . .' He stopped and placed a heavy hand on Anansi's shoulder. 'Just don't get your hopes up too much, OK?'

'But you'll try it?' asked Anansi, his eyes gleaming.

'I'll try it.'

'*Now?*'

'Now,' replied Rufaro. 'Just give me a moment. And you lot –' he gestured to the children – 'you all stand back. I have no idea what's going to happen next.'

Rufaro took the necklace from Red and moved out into the middle of the clearing. Then he snapped a thin branch off a tree and drew lots of strange magical shapes on the forest floor.

'How do you know all this stuff?' asked Anansi quietly.

Rufaro sighed. 'You know I said that when it came to fixing this curse I'd leave no stone unturned?'

Anansi nodded.

'Well, I learned all this looking under one of those stones,' said Rufaro. 'A *particularly* nasty stone. Now, Adeola, are you ready?'

'Ready as I'll ever be,' said Anansi's mum. She turned to walk towards her brother. Then she stopped and ran back towards Anansi, gathering him up into her arms. 'Just in case anything goes wrong,' she said smiling, even as a tear trickled down her cheek, 'I love you *so* much!'

'I know, Mum,' replied Anansi. 'You too.'

Adeola smiled as she let her son go and walked towards Rufaro who was placing the necklace in the middle of the shapes he'd drawn on the floor. He directed Adeola to stand in the centre of one circle while he stood in another. His face was pale and tight as he muttered a few words under his breath.

For a moment nothing happened. Everybody waited, tense and nervous.

Then, with the sound of fabric tearing, a thin ring of smoke shot out from the necklace and started spinning in a circle, growing bigger until it covered Rufaro, Adeola and all the magical symbols on the ground.

Through the smoke Red could just about see the outlines of Anansi's mum and uncle, but they looked fuzzy and unclear. The tearing sound continued, getting louder and louder until without warning it stopped. The cloud of smoke was swiftly sucked back into the necklace which flared with a black light and vanished – leaving behind nothing but a small cloud of cold blue mist, and two very surprised-looking people wearing clothes that were *far* too big for them.

'Mum!' yelled Anansi running forward. 'It's you, it really *is* you!'

14

A Taste of His Own Medicine

*E*arly the next morning, everyone was sitting under the Story Tree in the middle of Tale Town's Market Square. Hansel and Gretel had just finished telling everyone how they'd got lost on their camping trip in the woods and met a wild-eyed lady whose house was entirely made out of felt and organic vegetables. They'd been lucky to get away without being forced to

put on brightly coloured handmade jumpers or knit their own shoes.

As they were speaking, bright silver shoots grew out of the magical Story Tree, forever recording the adventure.

Ella and Cole were looking around happily. *Finally* they were free of the wicked witch of Squirrel-Nose Island and could come and go as they pleased. They were going to stay in Tale Town and Rapunzel had arranged for them to be guests in one of the many spare rooms at the castle — it really was *unbelievably* useful being a princess.

Once Hansel and Gretel had finished, the rest of the group took turns telling their parts of the wicked witch story, and Anansi was just explaining what had happened after everyone else had gone home.

'You'll never believe it . . .' he said. 'As soon as we walked into Rufaro's shelter out of the moonlight, they both turned back into trolls!'

'WHAaAT?' squawked Betsy, Red, Jack, Hansel, Gretel, Ella and Cole, all at once.

'I know!' replied Anansi. 'Crazy, right? Anyway, Rufaro worked out that the counter-spell only works in the moonlight. I guess if they'd cast the spell in the daytime it would have only worked in the sunlight. Either way, as the necklace turned to dust after Rufaro used it, we'll never know.'

'Oh, Anansi, I'm so sorry!' said Red.

'It's OK,' replied Anansi. 'At least
Mum's here now – besides, she's *still* my
mum – it doesn't matter what she looks
like!'

Red smiled and patted Anansi on the
back.

'Morning, small fry!' came a
voice, along with the sound
of squeaking wheels.

'Oh no . . .' groaned Jack.

Old Bert pulled his cart to a stop by the Story Tree and rubbed his grimy hands together. 'What's it to be today then? Fish-scale crisps? Or perhaps a bar of me new *Choc 'n' Squid* chocolate? Well, I say "chocolate", I wasn't exactly sure how to make chocolate . . . Still, whatever it is, it's brown.'

There was a long and awkward silence.

'OK, Bert,' said Red eventually. 'I'll have something.'

Old Bert's eyes lit up.

'Not again!' muttered Anansi, but Red ignored him.

'I'll take one of *everything* you've got!' she said.

Old Bert couldn't believe his luck. He quickly started taking out dirty pots and greasy old bags to stuff full of his unsavoury seafood snacks.

'But *only* . . .' added Red with a smile, 'if *you* eat them first, right here, in front of us.'

'B-b-b-but . . .' stammered Old Bert.

'Deal or no deal, Bert,' said Red, looking him straight in the eye.

'Can't say no to a sale,' muttered Bert. 'How hard can it be?'

'Eel-eye ice cream first, I think,' said Red.

'But it's all melted now!' protested Bert.

'Would you have sold it to me?' asked
Red.

'Well, yeah . . .'

'Go on then, tuck in!'

Bert glared at Red as he peeled the
grubby foil off a mushy cone filled with
soupy slush and *lots* of different sized
eel eyes. He lifted the cone to his lips,
determined to make the sale, and took
a big bite.

Seconds later his face went green,
his cheeks puffed up and, clutching his
grumbling stomach, Old Bert dashed
off, pushing his cart away as fast as he
could.

'Good work, Red,' said Anansi. 'You
had me going there for a minute!'

'Well, you know what?' said Red.

'Sometimes the person you have to trust the most is *yourself*. Anyway, all this adventuring's made me hungry,' she said. 'How about we go to Greentop's Cafe for something *proper* to eat?'

And so they walked through Tale Town in the bright morning sun – laughing and joking as they planned how to fill the brand new day.

The End

Red

Strengths:	Seeing the good in everyone
Weaknesses:	Seeing TOO MUCH good in everyone
Likes:	Wearing her favourite red hoody, having adventures, ice cream (as long as it's not fish-flavoured)
Dislikes:	Old ladies with long pointy ears and very sharp teeth

Rapunzel

Strengths:	Long, strong, magical hair that can tie itself in knots and be used to get out of (and into) trouble
Weaknesses:	Can be a bit self-absorbed
Likes:	Relaxing in a warm bath with an industrial-sized bottle of conditioner
Dislikes:	Knots, tangles, split ends, frizz, bad-hair days and – most of all – scissors!

Cole

Strengths: Enthusiasm!!! Why use one exclamation mark when you can use three?!

Weaknesses: As a Fairy Godbrother, Cole needs to brush up on the whole 'magic' thing

Likes: Fun! Jokes! Excitement! Exclamation marks – and Ella

Dislikes: Mean, boring, nasty witches; being bossed around

Ella

Strengths: Good at fixing clothes, carpets, bed-sheets, walls and . . . well, everything really

Weaknesses: A bit too keen to fix things that don't really *need* fixing

Likes: Cleaning, polishing, dusting, washing-up and her Fairy Godbrother Cole

Dislikes: The witch who's been keeping her prisoner, and Brussels sprouts

Look out for

Coming soon!

Little Legends are
also available from

Me Books